Hello, Family Members,

Learning to read is one of the most important accomplishments of early childhood. **Hello Reader!** books are designed to help children become skilled readers who like to read. Beginning readers learn to read by remembering frequently used words like "the," "is," and "and"; by using phonics skills to decode new words; and by interpreting picture and text clues. These books provide both the stories children enjoy and the structure they need to read fluently and independently. Here are suggestions for helping your child *before*, *during*, and *after* reading:

Before

- Look at the cover and pictures and have your child predict what the story is about.
- Read the story to your child.
- Encourage your child to chime in with familiar words and phrases.
- Echo read with your child by reading a line first and having your child read it after you do.

During

- Have your child think about a word he or she does not recognize right away. Provide hints such as "Let's see if we know the sounds" and "Have we read other words like this one?"
- Encourage your child to use phonics skills to sound out new words.
- Provide the word for your child when more assistance is needed so that he or she does not struggle and the experience of reading with you is a positive one.
- Encourage your child to have fun by reading with a lot of expression... like an actor!

After

- Have your child keep lists of interesting and favorite words.
- Encourage your child to read the books over and over again. Have him or her read to brothers, sisters, grandparents, and even teddy bears. Repeated readings develop confidence in young readers.
- Talk about the stories. Ask and answer questions. Share ideas about the funniest and most interesting characters and events in the stories.

I do hope that you and your child enjoy this book.

—Francie Alexander
Reading Specialist,
Scholastic's Learning Ventures

For my fourth-grade friend, Gayle
—K.M.

To "Biff" Heins
—M.S.

Go to www.scholastic.com for web site information on Scholastic authors and illustrators.

Library of Congress Cataloging-in-Publication Data
McMullan, Kate
Fluffy meets the dinosaurs / by Kate McMullan; illustrated by Mavis Smith.
p. cm. — (Hello reader! Level 3)
"Cartwheel books."
Summary: Fluffy the class guinea pig joins the students on a trip to the museum, where he carefully studies the exhibits and imagines tracing his ancestry back to the dinosaurs.
ISBN 0-590-52310-4
[1. Guinea pigs—Fiction. 2. Museums—Fiction. 3. School field trips—Fiction. 4. Dinosaurs—Fiction.] I. Smith, Mavis, ill. II. Title. III. Series.
PZ7.M47879F1c 1999
[E] —dc21 98-28798
CIP
AC

12 11 10 9 8 7 6 5 4 0/0 01 02 03 04

Printed in Mexico 24
First printing, March 1999

FLUFFY MEETS THE DINOSAURS

by Kate McMullan
Illustrated by Mavis Smith

Hello Reader!—Level 3

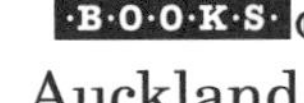

SCHOLASTIC INC.
New York Toronto London Auckland Sydney

Fluffy Rules!

Wade and Maxwell put Fluffy
in his play yard.
They put in lots of toy dinosaurs, too.
“Fluffy meets the dinosaurs!” said Wade.
Hey, dinosaurs, thought Fluffy.

"It is the age of the dinosaurs," said Wade.
"Dinosaurs rule the earth."
Those little things? thought Fluffy.
"Dinosaurs are fierce," said Maxwell.
"They are very, very powerful."
You must be joking, thought Fluffy.

Wade picked up a long dinosaur.
He stomped it around.
“I am thunder lizard!” he roared.
In your dreams, thought Fluffy.

Maxwell picked up a big-headed dinosaur.

He stomped it around.

“I am king of the dinosaurs!” he growled.

“T-rex rules!”

I don’t think so, thought Fluffy.

Maxwell made T-rex bite Wade's dinosaur.
Wade made his dinosaur roar.
The two dinosaurs began to fight.
Wade and Maxwell made strange
dinosaur noises with their mouths.
Soon more dinosaurs joined the battle.
Hey, watch the food dish! thought Fluffy.
You're messing up my play yard!
But the dinosaurs kept fighting.

“Math time!” called Ms. Day.

Wade and Maxwell put the dinosaurs down.

They went back to their seats.

Fluffy was alone with the dinosaurs.

Fluffy began running around his yard.

He kick-boxed the thunder lizard.

He took a flying leap
and stomped on T-rex.
He kept kicking and stomping.
Soon, not a dinosaur was left standing.

The age of dinosaurs is over,
Fluffy thought.
Now it is the age of guinea pigs.
Fluffy rules!

Fluffy's Great Adventure

"Today is our field trip
to the Natural History Museum,"
Ms. Day told her class.
"Did everyone bring a bag lunch?"
All the kids held up their lunch bags.

Wade put his lunch bag down.

He picked up Fluffy.

"We are going to a dinosaur museum!"

Wade told Fluffy.

Why not a Fluffy museum? thought Fluffy.

“Too bad you can’t come,” said Wade.

Who says I can’t? thought Fluffy.

And when Wade put him down for a second,

Fluffy crawled into Wade’s lunch bag.

Ms. Day's class rode a bus to the museum.
Everyone sat in a courtyard to eat lunch.
Wade opened his lunch bag
and took out his sandwich.
"Yuck!" he said.
Fluffy poked his head out of the bag.
Yuck? thought Fluffy. **It was yummy!**

“Yikes!” said Wade when he saw Fluffy.

“Ms. Day!” he called. “Look who’s here!”

“Fluffy!” exclaimed Ms. Day.

“How did you ever get into that bag?”

I’ll never tell, thought Fluffy.

"Our class pet Fluffy came with us,"
Wade told the museum guide.
The guide took Fluffy from Wade.
"What a pretty little cavy," he said.
Hey, watch your mouth! thought Fluffy.

"*Cavy* is the scientific name
for guinea pig," the guide explained.
"Let's go inside.
I'll show you Fluffy's cousins.
I'll show you his ancestors, which are
his great, great, great, great, great,
great, great, great, great grandparents."

Ms. Day's class followed the guide
into the museum.
They stopped by a glass case.
A sign on the case said RODENTS.
"Rodents are animals that like to gnaw,"
the guide said.
"They have very sharp front teeth.
Fluffy is a member of the rodent family."
Cool, thought Fluffy.

"Mice are rodents, too," the guide said.
"That means mice are Fluffy's cousins."
No way! thought Fluffy.
"So are rats," added the guide.
No, no, no! thought Fluffy.

Fluffy growled.

But the guide did not seem to notice.

He only walked to the next glass case.

“These are Fluffy’s ancestors,” he said.

“They came from South America.

They are called wild cavies.”

Wild! thought Fluffy. **That’s me!**

"Wild cavies were plump," the guide said.
"Bigger animals liked to eat them."
Hold it right there! thought Fluffy.

"Only cavies that hid did not get eaten," the guide went on. "They survived."

Fluffy looked into the case.

He saw two small furry animals hiding in the tall grass.

The animals looked very scared.

These are not my ancestors, thought Fluffy. **No way!**

The guide led the class down the hallway.
He stopped in front of a large statue.

Fluffy's eyes got very big.
Yes! he thought. **Here is my ancestor!**

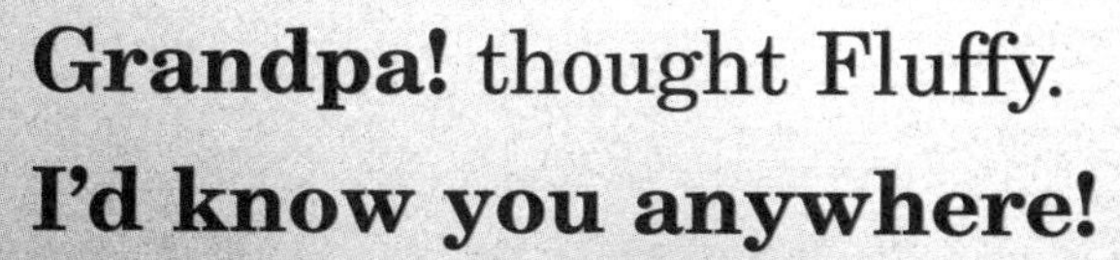

Grandpa! thought Fluffy.
I'd know you anywhere!

T-Fluffy

The guide showed Ms. Day's class
all sorts of dinosaur skeletons.
Some were huge.
Others were as small as lizards.
Some had horns.
Others had wings.
Big deal, thought Fluffy.

"No dinosaurs are alive today,"
the guide said.
"Why not?" asked Wade.
"Some scientists think that
millions of years ago,
a comet hit the earth," the guide said.
"It caused terrible dust storms.
The dust blocked out the sun.

Without sunlight, green plants died.
The dinosaurs had nothing to eat.
So they died, too.
Other scientists think flying dinosaurs
may have changed into birds.
But no one knows for sure."
I do! thought Fluffy. **I do!**

After a comet hit the earth,
tour guide Fluffy told his group,
most dinosaurs died. But not T-rexes.
They were too tough to die.

When dust from the comet
blocked the sun,
the Earth got cold. Brrrr!
It was an ice age.
So what did smart T-rexes do?
They grew fur coats!
Furry T-rexes survived the ice age.

For some reason, guide Fluffy went on,
fur never grew very well on T-rex tails.
So their tails froze and dropped off.
But who needs a tail?

Now, if there was one thing a T-rex loved, it was a big, juicy carrot. Luckily, carrots survived the ice age because they grew underground. T-rexes got down on all fours and dug up carrots all day long. Pretty soon T-rexes forgot that they ever ran around on their two back legs. T-rexes became four-legged creatures.

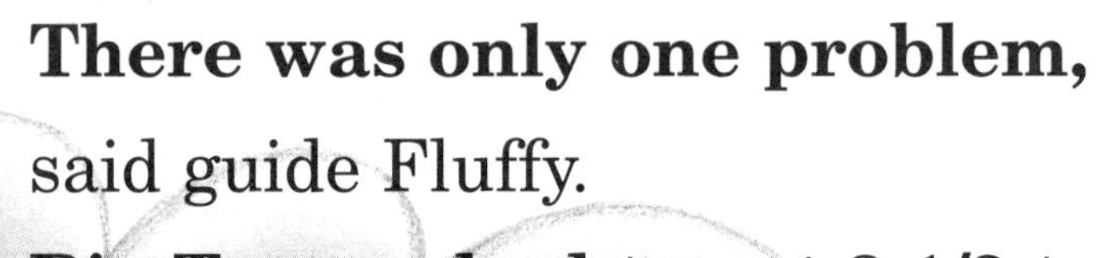

There was only one problem,
said guide Fluffy.
Big T-rexes had to eat 3 1/2 tons
of carrots every day just to stay alive.

It was hard work finding so many carrots.
But small T-rexes had it easy. They could fill up on just a few carrots.
So, over millions of years, T-rexes got smaller and smaller.
They ended up no bigger than grapefruits.
And they looked just like...

...me.

Mice and rats are rodents,

said guide Fluffy.

But a guinea pig's ancestors

go back to the age of dinosaurs.

Wade held Fluffy on the bus ride
back to school.
"I wish the dinosaurs were still around,"
he told Maxwell.
"Yeah," said Maxwell. "It would be cool
to have a dinosaur for a class pet."

Yeah, thought T-Fluffy.

Very cool!